anythir`

MICHAEL DAHL PRESENTS

The Haunted Dark

A TALE OF TERROR BY BRANDON TERRELL
ILLUSTRATED BY MARIANO EPELBAUM

STONE ARCH BOOKS
a capstone imprint

Michael Dahl Presents is published by Stone Arch Books,
A Capstone Imprint
1710 Roe Crest Drive
North Mankato, Minnesota 56003
www.mycapstone.com

Summary: Malik Jackson has never told anyone about his
terror of the dark. When his friend Ian dares him to join a
ghost-hunting mission in an abandoned mansion, Malik is
afraid he'll be laughed at if he backs down. Especially since
the girl he likes is part of the crew. Malik tells him himself
that if he stays in lighted rooms, if the flashlights have
enough batteries, if the power doesn't go out, he should be
fine. Right? Darkness is bad enough, but what about those
things inside the dark . . . things worse than Malik ever
imagined!

Library of Congress Cataloging-in-Publication Data is
available on the Library of Congress website.

ISBN: 978-1-4965-7343-8 (library hardcover)
ISBN: 978-1-4965-7347-6 (paperback)
ISBN: 978-1-4965-7351-3 (ebook PDF)

Printed in Canada.
PA020

MICHAEL
DAHL
PRESENTS

Michael Dahl has written about werewolves, magicians, and superheroes. He loves funny books, scary books, and mysterious books. Every Michael Dahl Presents book is chosen by Michael himself and written by an author he loves. The books are about favorite subjects like monster aliens, haunted houses, farting pigs, or magical powers that go haywire. Read on!

NYCTOPHOBIA

(nic-toh-FOH-bee-uh)

THE FEAR OF DARKNESS

EVERYONE IS AFRAID OF SOMETHING.

I'm afraid of quite a number of things. But a PHOBIA is a very special fear. It is deep and strong and long lasting. It is hard to explain why people have phobias—they just do.

In this frightening tale, Malik is forced to face his greatest fear on the night before Halloween. Which makes the story even scarier when I read it! Malik has kept his phobia a secret from everyone, including his best friends. But his friends will soon learn all about it—and wish they hadn't. The dark waits for all of them.

Michael Dahl

1

"What, are you *afraid* or something?"

My best friend Ian had his hands on his hips. He was looking at me with squinty, judgmental eyes. We were standing in the school hallway, about to head off to English class to listen to Mr. Hurley drone on and on about participle phrases.

"No, I'm not scared," I replied, slamming my locker closed for emphasis.

"Then why don't you want to explore a haunted house on the night before Halloween?" Ian asked. "I mean, that's the definition of a spooky good time, Malik."

"Because," I said. "The Rialto Theatre is screening the original *Invasion from Planet X* tonight."

Ian rolled his eyes. "That movie is so old," he said. "And the aliens are wearing fake-looking rubber masks."

I shrugged. "So? I like it. I thought you did too."

Ian scoffed. "Maybe when we were eight," he said.

Ian and I were twelve now, but we'd been friends since we were in daycare together. My mom liked to tell us we bonded over juice boxes and *Squirrel Detective* cartoons. Ever since then, it was like we'd been surfing the same brainwave.

Well, until now.

"You know what *is* scary?" Ian continued. "Hanging out with your older brother and his friends while they snoop around a haunted house."

"For the last time, I don't want to go to Croak Manor," I said. "We'd be trespassing, dude. And besides, if we show up when Tyrell and his friends are there, he'll kill me. Then *I'd* wind up haunting the place."

Croak Manor was an abandoned brick mansion on the edge of town. It used to be owned by a railroad tycoon named Bentley Gordon. Each year, Gordon would decorate for Halloween. He made it into a spooky haunted house for townspeople to visit. After he died, though, his estate closed it to visitors and left it abandoned.

Now, it just sits there, boarded up and covered with ivy. I'd heard stories about people going into Croak Manor and never coming out. I was convinced they were just ghost stories to frighten kids.

"Did you say something about Croak Manor?" someone behind me said.

I turned, and my heart began to thunder against my ribs.

It was Sasha Harris and her friend Claire Greene.

Sasha was the prettiest girl in our grade, no contest. She was also the most popular, the most athletic, and the most smartest . . . I mean, the *smartest*.

I opened my mouth to speak, but forgot how consonants and vowels worked.

Ian hadn't, though. "Yep!" he said. "Malik and I are going there tonight."

"For real?" Sasha shifted her weight onto her right hip, her textbooks nestled in the crook of her arm.

"For real," Ian said.

Sasha looked at Claire, and they seemed to talk with their eyes and not their mouths. They must have been surfing the same brainwave too.

Finally, Sasha looked back at us. "Can we join you?"

"Well, Malik here is being a bit of a fraidy-cat," Ian said, throwing me directly under the bus. "He hasn't decided if he can handle going or—"

"Sure I can," I blurted out. I didn't realize I was going to say it until the words snuck out of my mouth. "We're totally going."

Sasha smiled. "Good," she said. "Should we meet there around eight o'clock?"

Ian nodded. "Works for us."

"Well all right, then. Looking forward to it."

Sasha and Claire turned and walked away. They leaned their heads in close to one another, whispering as they went.

"See you at eight!" Ian shouted after them. A big smile was plastered on his face. Sure, he was excited to hang out with the girls. But he was also giddy because he'd gotten his way.

The bell rang, and the throng of kids in the hallway hurried off to class. My stomach twisted itself into a knot.

Ian slung one arm over my shoulder. "Malik," he said. "Tonight is gonna be a night you'll *never* forget!"

"Yeah," I muttered. "That's what I'm worried about."

2

I slipped out the front door of my house. The sun had dipped below the horizon, casting the sky in a dusky orange glow. My parents were inside watching a Halloween cartoon with my little sister. Tyrell had vanished just after dinner, practically inhaling his food to get out the door in time to meet his friends.

I didn't tell anyone about our plan to sneak over to Croak Manor.

"Can't believe I'm doing this," I muttered as I walked to Ian's house. The wind made the dead leaves on the sidewalk scuttle across my path. Jack-o'-lanterns gave me toothy grins from doorsteps.

Fake cobwebs and oversized stuffed spiders hung in windows and door frames. Scarecrows sat in lawn chairs. They seemed to watch me walk.

I put my head down and sped up.

Ian was sitting on the curb outside his house waiting for me. "Took you long enough," he said, checking his watch. "I thought maybe you'd chickened out and went to the movie instead."

"Unfortunately not," I said.

"Oh, come on," Ian said as we began to walk the half-mile across town. "Who knows? Maybe Sasha will get scared and ask to hold your hand."

He nudged me with an elbow to the ribs. Ian knew about my crush on Sasha. He'd figured it out one day after I'd spent an hour raving about her awesome volleyball skills in gym class.

"Knock it off," I said. I tried to keep the twitch of a smile from curling my lip.

By the time we reached the block with the Gordon mansion on it, the sky was dark. Pools of light from street lamps guided us. We stopped on the corner to wait for the girls to arrive.

In the distance, at the top of a small hill, sat the Gordon mansion. It looked like every scary house in every scary movie I'd ever watched. Ivy covered the brick exterior. Broken windows were covered with wood. A wrought-iron fence surrounded the property, overrun with spindly, dead bushes.

A chill ran up my spine. *What are we doing here?*

A whistle cut through the dark, and a pair of silhouettes walked toward us.

"Hey, guys!" Sasha called out.

She looked so cool, dressed in a black leather coat with her dreadlocks pulled up. I adjusted my own coat and tried to act calm.

"Hey!" Ian replied.

I could only wave.

"I used to ride my bike past this place all the time," Claire said quietly. "Never in the dark, though."

"Come on," Ian said. He eagerly led the way

up to the fence that surrounded the abandoned mansion. It took us a minute, but we found a spot in the fence where the iron was bent and we slipped through.

Huddled together, we walked toward the house. I peered at the windows that *weren't* broken, checking for light or movement. So far, there was no sign of Tyrell and his pals.

I bet they aren't even here.

"Oh, man. Is that a graveyard?" Ian asked.

To our left, along the side of the house and almost out of sight, was a small patch of grass. Sure enough, crumbling headstones stood like teeth jutting out of the ground. They were old and overgrown with weeds.

"Creepy," Sasha whispered.

The front door was hanging off its hinges, and was held in place by a pair of thick boards. When we reached it, Ian dug out his phone and turned on the flashlight app.

"Here we go," he said. Then he ducked under

the boards and slipped in through a small gap in the doorway without hesitation.

The girls followed—first Claire, then Sasha. Sasha looked back at me, smiled, and said, "Don't keep me waiting."

I took out my phone, turned on the flashlight, sucked in a deep breath, and plunged through the hole in the doorway.

3

Dust.

So. Much. Dust.

And cobwebs.

That was my first thought as I stepped inside
Croak Manor. The sweeping beams of our flashlights
picked up every speck of floating dust. It caked
the walls and hardwood floors. Spiderwebs hung
heavy in each corner, between the banisters of
the staircase, and around the metal chandelier
suspended from the ceiling.

We were in a foyer, an open room with a
twisting staircase against the far wall and a shadowy

hallway ahead. Other teenagers brave enough to sneak in had tagged the walls with graffiti. Colorful words and designs were sprayed on the peeling, warped wallpaper. One of the tags—*GO BACK NOW!*—made my skin crawl.

"This place is awesome." Ian spoke in a hushed voice, as if talking too loudly might wake something up that should really stay sleeping. Shadows bounced and shifted as we explored the area with our lights.

I peered down the darkened hall. Rooms with closed doors stretched along both sides.

"Whoa!" Sasha whispered. "Look at that!"

She had her head craned and was looking at something hanging above the twisting staircase. It was a painting coated with so much grime, it almost blended into the wall. The painting was a portrait of a scowling, heavyset man with wild eyes, drooping jowls, and a monocle in one eye. He was sitting in a chair. A long cane with a golden handle rested in his lap.

"Is that Bentley Gordon?" Claire asked.

"That'd be my guess," Ian said, shining his light up at the painting. "Maybe he's the one haunting the place." He cupped one hand around his mouth and yelled, "Mr. Gordon!? Hello?! Wanna come out and say hi?!" His voice echoed through the empty room.

Say hi . . . say hi . . . say hi . . .

"Shh! Quiet, Ian." Sasha wasn't really trying to hush him up. She was enjoying herself, which meant my chances of holding her hand were slim to big, fat none.

"So this place used to be a haunted house?" Claire whispered. "Like, a fake one? With people in masks jumping out at you?"

"A long time ago," Ian said. "Supposedly there's still stuff in here from then, like props and dummies and creepy things."

"Let's go find them," Sasha said.

She started walking up the steps, then stopped and turned. Her eyes grew wide.

I looked over at Ian and Claire. They had also

frozen like statues. And they were all staring at something behind me.

Before I could turn, something emerged from the shadowy hallway and clamped down hard on my shoulders!

4

I yelled at the top of my lungs, dropped my phone, and squirmed away from the shadowy claws gripping hard to my shoulders.

Only they weren't claws. They were hands.

My *brother's* hands.

Tyrell burst out laughing as he emerged from the shadows.

"Man, you just screamed like a little kid," Tyrell said. His two friends, Paige and Byron, came out of the hallway behind him. They were both pointing at me and laughing.

"Dude, that was *not* funny," I said, shoving him hard in the chest. I scooped my phone off the floor, flicked off the flashlight, and pocketed it.

Tyrell more than anyone knows how much I hate the dark. When we were younger, he pulled the cruelest prank on me. He hid under my bed, and when I curled up to go to sleep, he reached out—like he'd just done—and grabbed me. I was so scared, I started crying. Our parents grounded Tyrell. I wound up using a night-light for over a year because I couldn't fall asleep if it was too dark in my room.

"Come on," Tyrell said, shoving me back. "It was *kinda* funny."

"What are you guys doing here?" Byron asked.

"Same thing as you," Ian said. "We're looking for ghosts."

"Ha! Good luck." Paige said. "We've snooped all over this place and come up with nothing." She reached into her back pocket and removed a small device. She waved it around. "This cheap hunk of junk doesn't work at all."

Paige tossed the thing in my direction. It struck me in the chest, but I snagged it before it dropped.

"What is it?" Ian asked, coming up behind me. I held the device out. It looked like a remote for a television, except a little thicker. A row of small lights, from green to red, lined the top of it.

"It's an EMF reader," Paige explained. "It's supposed to measure electromagnetic waves."

"Which translates to 'it finds ghosts,'" Tyrell said bluntly. "Or their energy, at least. When the light's red, watch your back for spirits."

"And those lights haven't so much as blinked," Byron said. "So yeah, nothing here but a bunch of weird mannequins and stuff. We're blowing this joint."

He walked to the front door and slipped through the gap.

Paige followed him. But Tyrell stood his ground. "Come on," he said. "Let's go home."

Yes! Finally! I can use Tyrell as an excuse to leave

this place, I thought. I opened my mouth to respond, but Ian beat me to it.

"No way!" he blurted out. "We just got here!"

"And I told you, there ain't nothing to see," Tyrell said.

"I don't know, guys," I said. "I think . . ."

"I think we should stay," Sasha said. "What harm will it do? Tyrell says it's just a bunch of weird trash left over. Let's take a peek and then head out."

I looked over at Sasha. She wanted to stay. And I wanted to hang out with her. So I looked back at Tyrell and said, "We're good. You can go ahead without us."

Tyrell gave me one last look, as if to ask, "Are you sure?" Then he ducked out through the gap in the doorway.

We were alone.

"Come on," Sasha said, leading the way up the winding staircase.

At the top, we found another long hallway. The wood floor beneath us creaked with every step.

When we reached the first door leading off the hall, Sasha gripped the bronze handle, turned it, and pushed it open.

I could barely see a thing. A small sliver of moonlight broke through a pair of tall, dust-coated windows on the far side of the room. As my eyes adjusted to the darkness, I noticed something between them.

"What is that?" Ian asked as he crept up to it.

"I think . . . I think it's one of the old haunted house displays," I said.

From what I could see in the dim glow of our flashlights, there was a shelf with a bunch of antique-looking gadgets and glass bottles. A mannequin leaned against the shelf. And in front of him was a table with a sheet draped over it.

"It looks like a mad scientist's laboratory," I whispered.

"Really?" Sasha asked. She was right at my side. "I wish I could see it better."

And then, as if in response to her request, the display in front of us burst into bright, blinding life.

5

We all leaped back as the mad scientist's laboratory came alive. Lights hummed and glowed. An electrical current zapped between two metal beams above and behind the contraption. A hidden speaker played garbled audio of a person crazily laughing.

"What is going on?!" I shouted, covering my ears.

The mannequin of the mad scientist leaning against the shelf fell forward. It hit the table with the sheet. The figure under the sheet, the mad scientist's unseen creation, seemed to move.

"How is this possible?!" Claire asked. She cowered as the bolts of electricity continued to crackle from the display.

"I have no idea," I replied.

"I bet it's your brother pranking us again," Ian said. And then, like this was the only answer and therefore the truth, his shoulders sagged and he looked relieved. In fact, he was even smiling.

"Ha! Yeah, it has to be a prank," Sasha said. She walked up to the display.

"If it's a prank, then how is it moving?" I asked. "Cuz there's no way this place has working electricity."

"I don't know," Ian said. He was still enthralled by something that was way too freaky to be a prank. "Let's ask Tyrell. I bet he and his friends were only pretending to leave."

Ian walked back toward the hallway. Claire stood by the door, looking even more terrified than me. When Ian exited the room and went back into the hall, she quickly followed.

"Tyrell?" Ian called out.

No response.

"It really looks like a person," Sasha said. She was up close to the mad scientist now, poking at its face with one finger.

It really *did* look real. Its mouth was open in shock, its eyes wide. I wanted to tell Sasha to back up, but as I started to speak, the door behind us slammed shut.

"What the—?!" I blurted out.

Ian and Claire were still in the hall, leaving Sasha and me alone in the closed room. The door rattled as Ian pounded on it from the other side.

"Hey!" I heard him call out. "What did you do that for?!"

I raced to the door and tried the handle. It didn't budge. "I didn't do anything!"

"Well, neither did I!" Ian called out.

"Malik, check it out," Sasha said as she came up behind me. She pointed to the EMF reader in my back jeans pocket. I'd kind of forgotten it was there. I pulled it out and watched it light up like a Christmas tree, all the way from green to red.

"Whoa," I said, glancing at the display . . .

. . . just as it all went dark again.

The display. The EMF reader. The world.

Dark.

Startled, Sasha cried out and grabbed my arm. An afterimage of the bright glow of the mad scientist laboratory danced and swirled in my eyes. I couldn't see a thing anymore.

Ian knocked again. "What's going on?" he shouted.

"The lights," I explained. "They're out again."

In the silence that followed our exchange, a noise began to drift toward us in the dark. I strained to hear it.

"What is that?" Sasha whispered.

"Shh!"

The sound was rhythmic. A soft scrape, followed by a tap on the floor. Scrape, *tap*. Scrape, *tap*. Scrape . . . *tap*.

"Guys?" Ian said. He sounded terrified. "I think someone's out here with us."

"Stop messing around!" I said. "Tyrell! Knock it off!" I didn't know if it was my brother. But I had to plead to him anyway, just in case.

Scrape . . . *tap.*

"Ian? Claire?" I pounded my fist on the door. *"IAN?!"*

Nothing.

It was like they'd vanished.

"We have to get out of here," I said. My eyes were adjusting. The white dots faded. I could finally make out the shape of things—the windows and the darkened display.

"There," Sasha said. She had her phone in one hand, using it as a flashlight again, and was pointing it across the room. Near the corner, almost hidden, was another doorway. She pulled me by the arm, leading me toward it.

This door wasn't locked. It swung right open.

"What do we do?" Sasha asked.

I took out my own phone again and turned on the flashlight app. Light blazed through the doorway at the blackness beyond.

"We have to find Ian and Claire," I said.

And together we rushed through the doorway.

The moment we stepped into the next room, light shone in our faces and made us squint. In fact, many dazzling bursts of light washed across the room, moving as one every time we swept our arms from side to side.

I jumped back, startled.

"Mirrors," Sasha whispered, unfazed.

She was right. The room was filled with mirrors. Large ones, small ones, long and short. They hung from the walls and stood upright throughout the room. Each reflected our shadows and the glow from the phones in our hands.

A maze of mirrors. And we were caught in the middle.

"The door to the hallway must be this way," Sasha said. She pulled me along by the arm as I kept staring at my reflection in the mirrors.

"Oof!" My shoulder slammed into a full-length mirror held up in a thick wooden frame. My phone slipped out of my hand. The light and shadows twisted as it fell to the floor.

Sasha let go of my arm as I bent down to pick up my phone. She kept moving. "I see the door," she said. "It's over here."

I started after her. Only now, it was like the mirrors were moving in on me. Like they were trying to trap me. *That's a dumb thing to think,* I told myself. *Mirrors can't move.*

"Where are you?" I asked, peering around the closest mirror, hoping to follow Sasha's voice.

"By the door," she replied. Her voice sounded like it was coming from every direction. I could faintly see the glow of her flashlight above the mirrors in front of me. I started in that direction.

That's when I heard it again.

Scrape . . . *tap*. Scrape . . . *tap*. Scrape . . . *tap*.

"Whatever weird prank this is," I said loudly, "I'm ready for it to end. You can come out now, Tyrell!"

There was a flicker of movement directly in front of me. I leaped back in surprise. A large mirror held my reflection, showing my scared face lit by the glow from my flashlight.

Until a dark shadow in the shape of a person slithered out from behind my reflection.

I spun around to face the weird shape . . . and saw nothing.

"Sasha?" We needed to get out of here. I was seeing things in the dark now.

Sasha didn't answer.

"Hello?" I peered over the mirrors in front of me, where the door and Sasha had to be. Only the light was gone now. *She* was gone.

I was alone.

I wove through the maze of mirrors, trying to

find the door. It felt like I was walking in circles, like I was lost in a forest and the trees all looked the same. I shoved one of the mirrors out of frustration, pushing it aside. The mirror toppled over and smashed with a loud, tinkling sound that echoed in my ears.

Shards of glass lay at my feet, each sparkling in the glow of my flashlight. When I looked beyond them, I noticed that in the space left by the fallen mirror, I could see the door to the hallway.

"Finally," I said, breathing a sigh of relief.

And that was when the light on my phone completely winked out.

7

"No, no, no!" I smacked my phone into the palm of my hand, wishing and hoping the flashlight would turn back on.

No luck. My phone was dead.

For a minute, I didn't move. I just closed my eyes and tried to take deep, calming breaths. I couldn't, though, because all I kept seeing was Tyrell reaching out from under my bed and grabbing me by the shoulders like he did earlier tonight. I could feel the tears starting to come, but I pushed them down. Crying wouldn't help right now.

I tried to remember where the gap in the mirrors had been, and which direction I needed to walk to reach the door. I took a step. Mirror shards crackled under my shoe.

Looks like I'm gonna have seven years of bad luck, I thought.

If it meant getting out of here, I'd take the bad luck.

More small steps, more crunched glass. My eyes were adjusting to the dark. I could see the outlines of a few mirrors on either side of me. With my arms in front of me like I was a shambling mummy or zombie, I edged forward.

Thunk.

The cold wood of the door against the palm of my hand. I'd made it. The hallway was just beyond. I found the handle and swung the door open.

"Sasha! Ian! Claire!" I called, stepping into the hall.

But it wasn't the hallway.

It was another dark room.

"Wait . . . what?" I could have sworn this would be the hallway.

A large picture window let in enough light for me to see the spacious, hollow room. It looked almost the same as the previous one. But instead of being cluttered with mirrors, this room was empty except for a huge, tattered rug on the floor and a chandelier hanging from the ceiling.

I hurried over to the window bathed in moonlight. *Maybe Tyrell and his friends are still out front*, I thought. *I can get their attention.*

I looked out the window, fully prepared to start banging on the glass with my fists.

The view was not what I expected. The window did not look out toward the front of the house. Instead I was staring down at the small, cluttered cemetery we'd seen as we approached the mansion.

"No way," I said. My whisper sounded like a scream in the silence. *The cemetery should be on the other side of the house,* I thought. I felt like a lab rat in a maze trying to find a hunk of cheese.

Clouds swallowed the moon, cutting the light in the room to a dusky darkness again.

"Malik?"

The voice was soft, but clearly Sasha's.

I spun around. "Sasha!" I was so relieved to see her. Her silhouette stood on the far side of the room. "Where have you been?" I crossed the room as quickly as possible without tripping in the dark.

"Looking for you," Sasha said, her voice still timid.

"Did you find Ian and Claire?" I asked.

"No."

"It's OK," I said. "We can find them together. Did your phone die too?"

"Yes."

I made it across the room to Sasha. I wanted to hug her, even though we'd only been separated for a few moments. So much weird stuff had been happening, it felt like we'd been in Croak Manor for a lifetime.

I didn't hug her, but I *did* reach out for her, to

let her know that we were safe now that we were together again. I slid my hand into hers.

She was cold. Freezing.

Stiff.

Wait a second . . .

The clouds broke, and moonlight flooded down once more through the large picture window, casting away the shadows around Sasha.

Only, it wasn't Sasha staring back at me.

It was a wide-eyed, grinning mannequin!

8

The mannequin looked lifelessly at me, its mouth peeled back in a devilish grin. I immediately drew back my hand, afraid that the dummy wouldn't let me go. I could see the door behind it, open now.

And then came the sound.

Scrape . . . *tap*. Scrape . . . *tap*.

With a full-throated holler, I rushed at the mannequin, knocking it over like a defensive tackle taking down a quarterback. The mannequin clattered to the floor. Its creepy, grinning head was knocked off its body, and it rolled off into the shadows. I ran into the hallway.

Darkness in both directions.

Which way are the stairs?

Behind me, the door banged shut.

There's dark . . . and there's *dark* dark. So dark you can't see your hand waving an inch in front of your face. I was swimming in that kind of blackness now.

I raised my arms out again, doing that zombie shuffle down the hall. As I did, my foot kicked something and sent it skittering across the wooden floorboards.

"That sounded like a phone," I said to myself. I hoped that talking aloud, even if no one was there, would make it easier to be alone in the dark.

It didn't.

I got down on my hands and knees and searched the floor for whatever it was I kicked. Dust and grit coated my palms and fingers. When I found the thing, I realized it wasn't a phone at all. It was the EMF reader Sasha had been carrying. She must have dropped it when she . . . vanished.

"No!" I barked out in frustration. I stood up and sighed. "Now what?" I asked the dark.

Scrape . . . *tap*. Scrape . . . *tap*.

The noise was coming from in front of me. It was followed by a quiet creak of floorboards.

I wasn't alone in the hallway.

In my hand, the lights of the EMF reader began to flicker. Green first . . . then up to yellow . . . then red.

Scrape . . . *tap*. Scrape . . . *tap*.

Every hair on my neck stood on end. Goosebumps rolled like waves down my arms.

I turned, and with the EMF reader in front of me, started to walk as fast as possible. I slid along the wall, stumbling, catching myself, moving on. I could hear the noise behind me.

Scrape . . . *tap*. Scrape . . . *tap*.

Ahead, hard to see at first but slowly coming into focus, was dim orange light. I kept moving along the hall toward it. The noise behind me was gone, but I wasn't about to stop.

I saw the stairs about a second before I stumbled down them. My feet skidded to a stop. It was a wooden staircase with a banister, like the first set we climbed. The orange glow was coming from below.

It took me about a split second to make up my mind.

I quickly stumbled down the stairs, heading toward the flickering light.

Step by step, the orange glow grew, but I couldn't see exactly where it was coming from.

Each step cracked and groaned.

Twenty steps, then thirty, forty. I counted each one under my breath. When my friends and I had climbed the stairs to the second floor, there had only been a handful. I realized this staircase wasn't taking me back to the main level.

I was heading toward the basement.

There was a small landing at the bottom of the stairs. It was dank and musty. Cold, too. The orange light was coming from a thick glass window set into a door in front of me. It was the only room down here.

For a minute, I considered running back up the stairs. But it was pitch black up there, and I had already been lost inside the mansion's confusing rooms.

So I took my chances and shoved open the door with my shoulder.

The temperature shift was intense, swinging from cold to hot so quickly my breath caught in my throat and I started to cough. In the center of the room was a massive, iron furnace whose belly glowed brightly from a large rectangular hole. Flames licked its insides. Like the mad scientist laboratory upstairs, I wondered how it was possible for the furnace to be operational.

But I didn't think about it for long. Because my attention immediately shifted to what else I saw.

Mannequins.

A whole bunch of them.

They stood in clusters around the furnace, all

shapes and sizes. Men. Women. Children. Like the mannequins upstairs, they looked lifelike. Each held an expression of shock, of surprise, of fear. White sheeting was draped over several of them, making them look like ghosts.

They were huddled around the furnace as if they were trying to stay warm.

Scrape . . . *tap*. Scrape . . . *tap*.

From the depths of the boiler room, the sound came again.

I froze, unable to turn, unable to escape. And really, what escape was there anymore? It was like the house had led me here, like I was always supposed to come to this boiler room.

Scrape . . . *tap*.

Deep in the room, beyond the ancient steel structure and its tentacle-like arms, a shadow appeared in the orange light cast on the wall. It grew into a shape, a person's shadow standing in the depths of the room. The person was holding what looked like a cane.

And with each step the shadow took, the cane slid across the floor, then rapped against it.

Scrape . . . *tap*. Scrape . . . *tap*.

A deep-throated, scratchy laugh filled the room.

Whoompf.

The furnace went out, taking with it the orange glow, the heat. The light. A cold chill coursed through me. The EMF reader in my shaking hand was now the only light.

It blazed bright red.

10

The mannequins began to move.

Their feet shuffled like a horde of zombies. Their rigid arms creaked. I felt a hand brush against me. Then another. The EMF reader was going berserk. I chucked it across the room and heard it shatter against the iron furnace.

The shadow's laughter echoed through the darkness.

"I am not dying in Croak Manor," I said with authority.

Turning, I stumbled forward to the stairs. They were right where I thought, and I quickly began to climb. My feet pounded up the steps. I slid my hand along the wall for support. As I went, my left foot missed a step, and I fell forward on the staircase. I barely had enough time to get my hands out in front of me before I struck the stairs hard.

"Oof!" Pain shot through my arms and hands. I fought it off, stood, and kept climbing. I could feel my whole body shaking.

Finally, I reached the top step and found the hallway. But it wasn't the hallway I'd come from. A boarded-up window was to my left, a sliver of moonlight peeking through it. I hurried over and peered through the slats with one eye.

The yard. The street. A pool of light from a street lamp.

I was on the main level. Which meant the foyer was ahead of me.

I broke into a cautious run down the hall. Wallpaper flaked off in my fingers every time I touched the walls. Cobwebs stuck to my hands and in my hair.

I turned a corner.

And there was the foyer. Right ahead, bathed in dusky light.

Three figures stood there waiting.

Three figures I recognized instantly.

"Guys!" I shouted. "Ian! Sasha! Claire! Over here!"

It was them. I could see them peering down the hall, looking for me.

I ran full-speed toward them.

When I broke into the foyer, I was gasping for air. I bent over, my hands on my knees, trying to catch my breath. "Guys . . ." I said. "So glad . . . to see . . . you're—"

I looked up at Ian.

And a mannequin of my best friend stared back at me.

"No!"

Sasha and Claire had been turned into mannequins too. Their faces waxy, their arms and legs rigid, like the ones in the boiler room.

The truth struck me then, and I whispered, "They were all real people."

Every mannequin in the place was once a real person who'd dared to step inside Croak Manor.

The portrait of Bentley Gordon stared down at me. Bentley Gordon, sitting in a chair, holding—

"A cane," I whispered.

I thought about the seats of the Rialto Theatre, so comfortable and cozy. The popcorn, buttery and delicious. I thought about my family—my dad and sister probably reading bedtime stories, my mom sewing my Halloween costume for tomorrow night. I thought of Ian, who told me last week we were too old to trick or treat but who wanted to go anyway. Sasha and Claire, whose curiosity brought out courage in me I didn't know I had. Tyrell, giving me a look that said it was OK if I wanted to leave, that he was sorry for scaring me.

I thought of it all as I stood there, stiff as the mannequins of my friends around me.

The foyer was growing dark.

I thought of the graffiti on the wall—*GO BACK NOW*—and how we should have heeded its advice.

It grew darker.

The sound of Bentley Gordon's ghostly cane echoed through the foyer.

Scrape . . . *tap.* Scrape . . . *tap.* Scrape . . .

tap.

GLOSSARY

berserk (bur-ZERHK)—out of control with excitement or anger

brainwave (BRAYN-wayv)—an idea or way of thinking

devilish (DEH-vuhl-ish)—something evil

electromagnetic (i-lek-troh-mag-NET-ik)—of, relating to, or produced by electromagnetism

emphasis (EM-fuh-siss)—to give more importance to something

estate (eh-STATE)—a large piece of land, usually with a large house on it

foyer (FOI-ur or foi-AY)—an entrance hall, especially of an apartment building or big house

graffiti (gruh-FEE-tee)—pictures or words spray-painted on buildings, bridges, and trains

heeded (HEE-ded)—noticed or paid attention to something

judgmental (juhj-MENT-ahl)—an opinion of something or someone

mannequin (MAN-ih-kin)—a life-sized model of a human

scuttle (SKUH-tuhl)—to move or run as if in a hurry

silhouette (sil-oo-ET)—an outline of something that shows its shape

FACE YOUR FEAR!

Now that you've read the story, it's no longer only inside this book. It's also in your brain. Can your brain help you answer the prompts below?

1. If you were visiting Croak Manor, what would you do differently? Would you be able to escape? Would you bring any other equipment with you?

2. Imagine you had Paige's EMF reader to find ghosts. Write about how the EMF reader might react to a spooky place in your town.

3. Discuss some clues given earlier in the story that reveal the strangeness of Croak Manor and its mannequins.

4. How did Malik let peer pressure influence his decision to go to Croak Manor at night? Talk about how things could have gone differently if he went by his own feelings.

5. Malik had to try to escape on his own after everyone else had been changed. Discuss how you would have felt if you were in his position.

FEAR FACTORS

nyctophobia (nic-toh-FOH-bee-uh)—the fear of darkness

Fear of the dark is one of the most common fears felt by humans. It is easy to get lost in the dark. Familiar surroundings look different at night than they do during the day. These factors make people uneasy or even fearful of darkness.

People who suffer from nyctophobia are terrified of what they *think* might be hiding in the darkness. Since they can't see any real danger in the dark, their imaginations create possible dangers and frightful situations that *could* occur. They're certain that something awful waits just out of sight!

A child's fear of the night could be connected to the fear of monsters in the closet, or under the bed—both dark places.

Dark, spooky houses are a feature of hundreds of stories, movies, and television shows. Again, because almost all of us have this fear, we can relate, or sympathize with the heroes in a story about the dark. In fact, one of the first scary films ever made was called *The Old Dark House* (1932).

Darkness is often associated with bad stuff. Think of Darth (sounds like dark!) Vader's pitch-black uniform. Or the dark Ringwraiths on their nightmare horses in *Lord of the Rings.* Or Voldemort's billowing black cape. Or the dark button eyes of the "other mother" in *Coraline.* Creepy!

In folklore and legends, the one power that can defeat creatures of the night is sunlight. Vampires burn to ash when light touches them. The ghostly dementors of the Harry Potter books disappear when a burst of magical light shines on them. And werewolves can only be defeated by silver bullets—silver, a bright, shiny metal that reflects light.

ABOUT THE AUTHOR

Brandon Terrell has been a lifelong fan of all things spooky, scary, and downright creepy. He is the author of numerous children's books including several volumes in Capstone's Spine Shivers and Snoops, Inc. series. When not hunched over his laptop writing, Brandon enjoys watching movies (horror movies, especially!), reading, baseball, and spending time with his wife and two children in Minnesota.

ABOUT THE ILLUSTRATOR

Mariano Epelbaum is a character designer, illustrator, and traditional 2D animator. He has been working as a professional artist since 1996, and enjoys trying different art styles and techniques. Throughout his career Mariano has created characters and designs for a wide range of films, TV series, commercials, and publications in his native country of Argentina. In addition to Michael Dahl Presents: Phobia, Mariano has also contributed to the Fairy Tale Mix-ups, You Choose: Fractured Fairy Tales, and Snoops, Inc. series for Capstone.

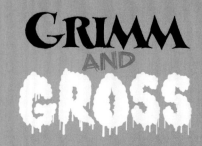

GRIMM AND GROSS

only from capstone